Austin Conboy lives in Ireland with his beautiful wife and three children, Oz, Poppy and Penny. This is his first children's book written after many nights spent making up bedtime stories and his children persuading him to "please write them down, Daddy".

The book is about his love of animals, caring for the environment and making his children proud.

Diana Princess of Whales

illustrated by Damian Whelan

AUSTIN CONBOY

AUSTIN MACAULEY PUBLISHERS™

LONDON * CAMBRIDGE * NEW YORK * SHARJAH

A CIP catalogue record for this title is available from the British Library.

ISBN 9781398401259 (Paperback)
ISBN 9781398401266 (Hardback)
ISBN 9781398401273 (ePub e-book)

www.austinmacauley.com

First Published (2021)
Austin Macauley Publishers Ltd
25 Canada Square
Canary Wharf
London
E14 5LQ

This book is dedicated to my wife, Deborah, and my amazing kids, Oz, Poppy and Penny. Thanks for everything guys!

I would like to thank Damian Whelan for his amazing art work and my wife and family for their support.

Deep in the bluest beautiful ocean live a royal
family and their beautiful daughter
And this is their story...

Each day the king carefully spent his time inspecting his Kingdom, especially making sure that the turtles had shined their shells, the seahorses had cleaned out their stables and most importantly, that the crayfish had put away their crayons..

9

However one particular day something didn't feel right. With that the King heard the saddest cry and went to investigate. The cry was coming from dirty dump zone, the one part of the Kingdom where no one dared to enter. In the middle of all the nasty plastic and dumped rubbish (that silly human people had not put into the correct recycle bins) was a scared but beautiful baby Narwhal, which would change his life forever.

He brought the baby back to the Queen who when she saw her immediately fell flipper over tail in love with her new little princess, we shall call her Diana, the queen said triumphantly.

Diana grew quickly and always found it very easy to make friends, but her best friend of all was an Orca named Oli. He was the biggest, strongest and fastest of all her friends and always looked out for the princess no matter what trouble she got into. However as Diana grew so did her tusk and this it seemed was the cause of a lot of her problems.

She loved playing with her friends but she always seemed to ruin the games. One day while playing tailball, Diana burst the last ball with her pointy tusk, all her friends were so annoyed and poor Diana could not take it anymore, why do I have to be so different to everyone she thought. So she swam and swam as fast as she could and did not look back, she swam until she could not longer hear her upset friends.

When all of a sudden she heard a cry for help, and just like her father the King did before she followed that cry. It took her to the one place in the kingdom where she was very frightened of, the Dirty dump zone. In amongst some plastic wrapping and discarded old fishing net she spotted Tommy the Turtle, he was tired, tangled and very scared. Diana did not know what to do but as always Oli had followed her and was there to save the day. But when Oli went in to help Tommy he got caught up in the net also. Diana had to think fast, Tommy and now Oli were running out of time.

And with that it came to her, she swam head first into where Tommy and Oli were and with her big pointy tusk she cut through the tangled mess like a hot knife through butter. She had done it, Diana had saved the day.

From that day on Diana was seen as a hero, she also made a promise to herself never to worry about being different, sometimes being different is what makes you special..
Even if sometimes she still burst the ball.
That is the start of the adventures of Diana the Princess of Whales